Soaring to the

Gary M. Prior/Allsport

Mike Powell/Allsport

Imagine traveling swiftly down a snowy mountain using only two poles and two narrow pieces of wood or metal. The wind chills your face. Snow flies up at you. People cheer for you. You are a skier.

To enjoy skiing, you must enjoy the cold. Wherever there is snow there are cold temperatures! There are three kinds of ski competitions at the Olympics. These events are **Alpine, Nordic,** and **Freestyle.** Men and women compete separately in these events.

Nathan Bilow/Allsport

Alpine skiing is for the skier who enjoys going fast. There are five events for the racers. These races are the **downhill, slalom, giant slalom, super giant slalom,** and **combined.** The racers must be fearless of steep slopes and fast speeds. They must be risk-takers.

Mike Powell/Allsport

Mike Powell/Allsport

At the top of the downhill slope, the racer prepares for take-off. The clock starts, and the race begins. The skier goes so fast that many objects become a blur. The only thing on the skier's mind is to have a faster time than any of his or her opponents. The skier must stay focused and in control during the downhill speed race. A racer can reach speeds of up to 80 miles per hour (128 kilometers). That is really fast! Sometimes, the skier even becomes airborne.

Mike Powell/Allsport

Another type of Alpine event is the **slalom.** It is also a downhill race, but the skiers must zigzag back and forth instead of going straight. The skiers must stay focused as they ski through gates. They cannot miss a gate or fall, otherwise they will be disqualified. They know that one wrong turn will cause them to wipe out!

Mike Powell/Allsport

The **giant slalom** is like the slalom, but it is steeper, faster, and longer. It has fewer turns. The turns are smoother and wider. The skiers must be brave to compete in this challenging event. Since speed is one key to winning, they must practice for hours each day on different types of slopes. By practicing a lot, the skiers become more comfortable and confident about competing!

Shaun Botterill/Allsport

The **super giant slalom** is like the downhill and the giant slalom but even longer. People love to watch this event. The skiers must have a lot of strength and endurance. This means that they must be in great shape. They also have to eat healthy. The skiers use speed and control to win this difficult race.

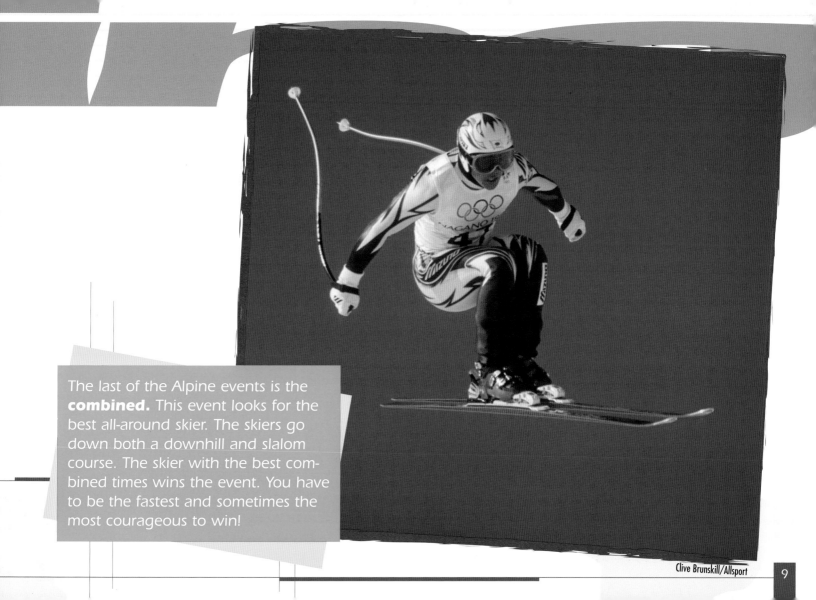

The last of the Alpine events is the **combined.** This event looks for the best all-around skier. The skiers go down both a downhill and slalom course. The skier with the best combined times wins the event. You have to be the fastest and sometimes the most courageous to win!

Clive Brunskill/Allsport

Al Bello/Allsport

Competing in the Nordic **cross-country** event requires muscle strength and endurance. Skiers race for miles as they push their skis through the snow.

Other Nordic events are **ski jumping** and the **Nordic combined.** These events challenge the skier in different ways. Skiers must be in great shape to compete. They must be risk-takers!

Craig Jones/Allsport

In **ski jumping,** the skiers go down a slide-like surface and then take off. They place their bodies in a coiled position so they can thrust themselves forward and into the air. Ski jumpers use balance and coordination to help them soar through the air. They soar about 10 feet (3 meters) in the air but cover more than a football field in length. Ski jumpers fly for 4 to 5 seconds before landing. They must keep their knees straight and be stable. When they land, they try not to let their hands touch the snow. Ski jumpers must be steady, be fearless, and stay in control.

The **Nordic combined** event combines cross-country with ski jumping. The event takes two days. One day is for each part. The Nordic skier has to stay motivated and focused both days. He or she must have both explosive power and endurance. It is the ultimate test for a skier!

Mike Powell/Allsport

Freestyle skiing is another competition for the Olympic skier. There are two parts of freestyle competition: **aerials** and **moguls.** Moguls are bumps in the snow and can be over 3 feet (1 meter) tall. When skiers compete in the mogul event, they must race at high speeds. They have to make quick short turns and must stay in control. The skiers are judged on speed and on how well they complete their turns. They make sure to keep their knees bent to keep from getting hurt. With such a bumpy race, the moguls put a lot of pressure on the skier's knees.

The aerial event is the other part of the freestyle competition. The skiers take off down a hill. They hit a snow-packed jump and are launched into the air. As they fly up to 50 feet (4.5 meters) in the air, they do flips, twists, and somersaults. Their landing is very important because any mistake could mean an injury. The jumps look scary and exciting!

Nathan Bilow/Allsport

A skier needs a lot of practice and perseverance to make it to the Olympic Games. To become a champion, a skier must be daring, dedicated, and determined!